My Grandfather's Masbaha

Written by
Susan Daniel Fayad

Illustrated by
Avery Liell-Kok

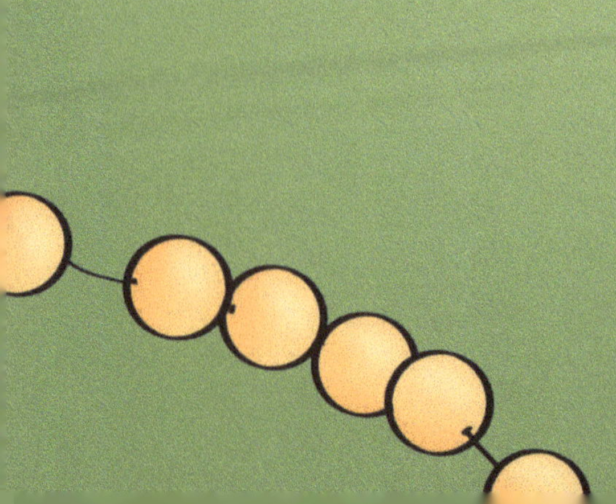

ISBN: ISBN:978-0-692-29201-3
Publication Date:9/8/2014

Library of Congress Control Number: 2013917619

In loving memory of

Yousef Daniel

-- he was our greatest blessing.

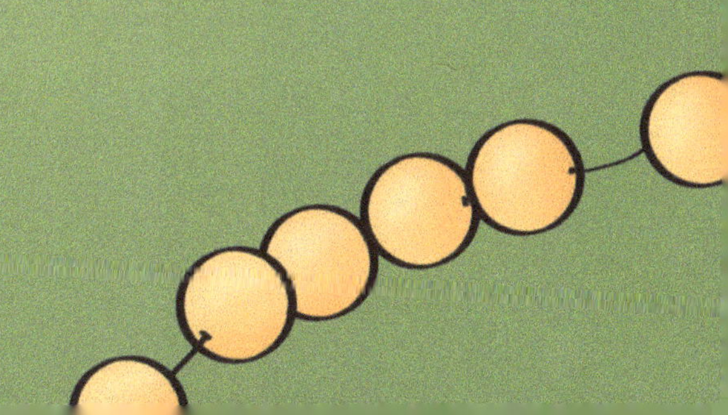

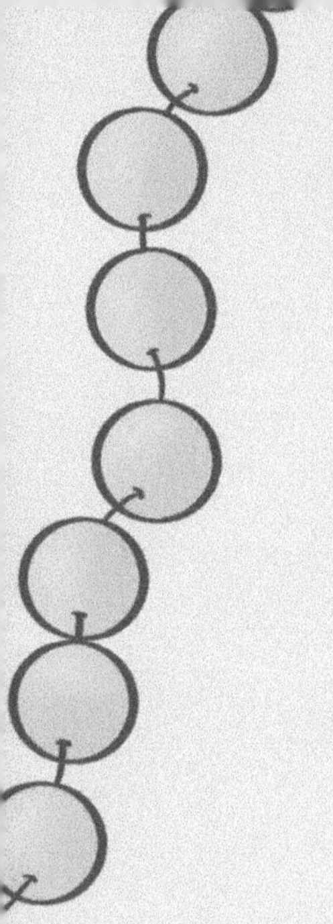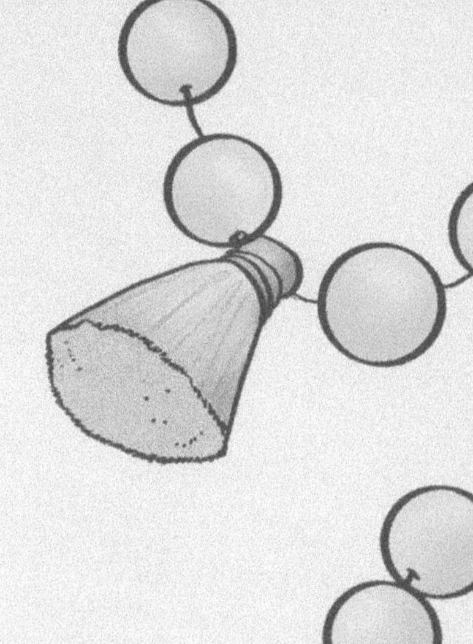

It was a summer day in Lebanon. Adam was visiting his grandparents (Jidoo and Sitoo) in their hometown of Bakeefa.

"Urgh! Stomp! Stomp!"

Adam came into the house huffing and puffing, gritting his teeth, squinting his eyes, and squeezing his fists. The little giant declared, "I'm so mad. My friends left. I have nothing to do. I have not toys and no fun. I don't have anything!"

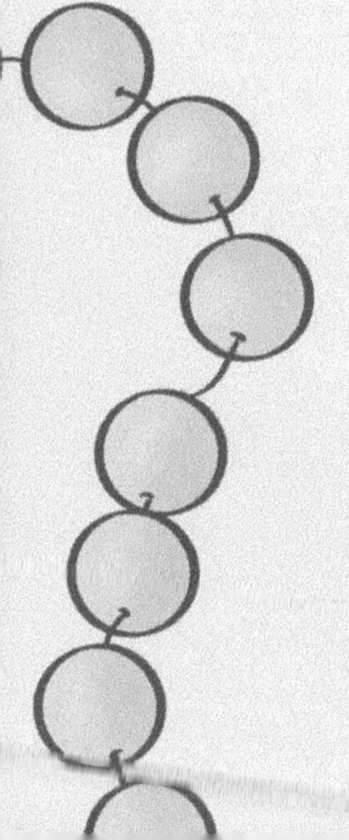

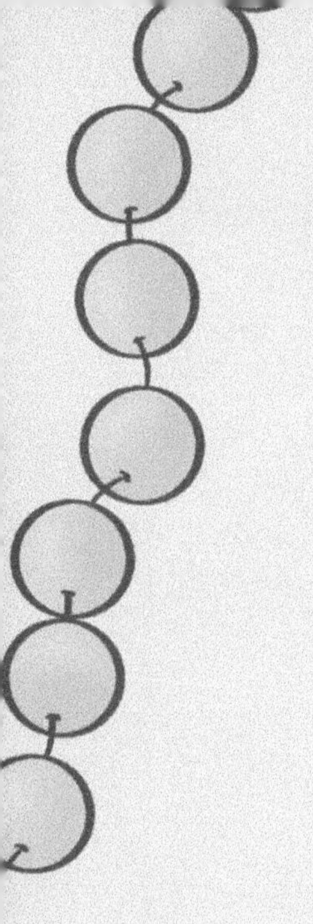
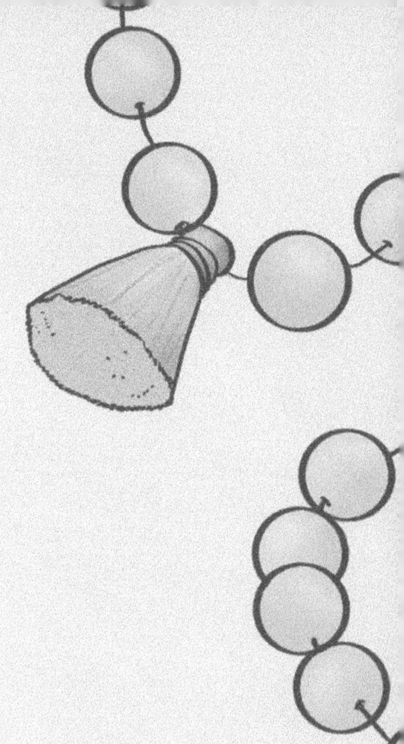

"Ha ha, ha ha," chuckled Adam's grandfather. His belly rolled more and more with each laugh.

Adam's face became redder and redder and was going to burst at any minute. "Jidoo Yousef!" Adam called out to his grandfather, "Why are you laughing at me?!"

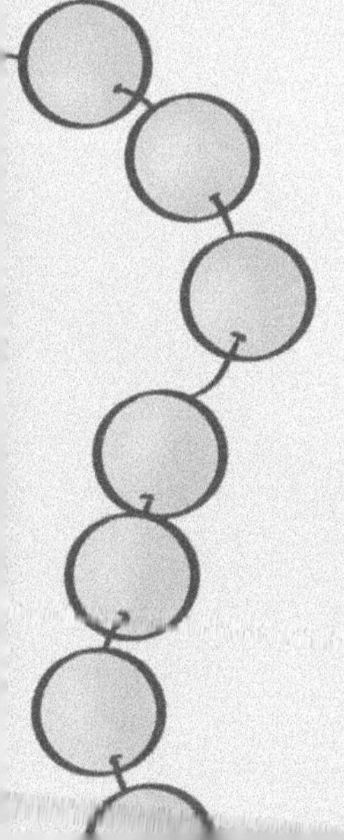
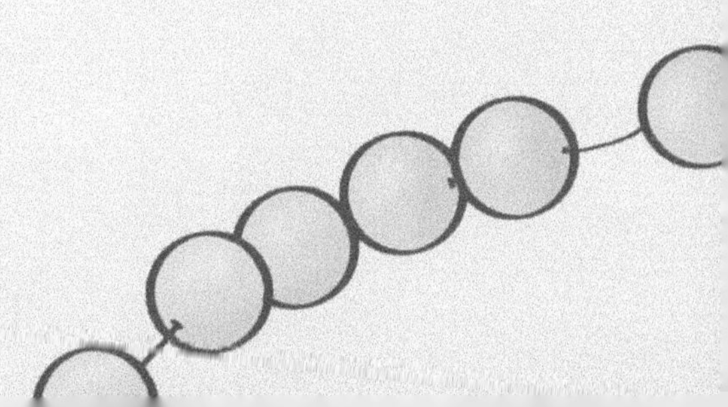

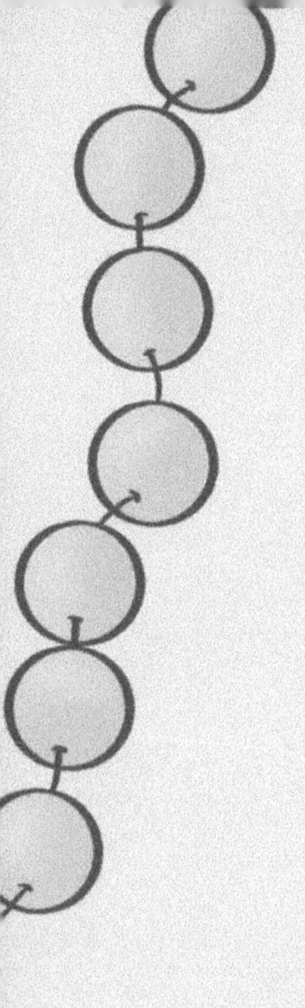
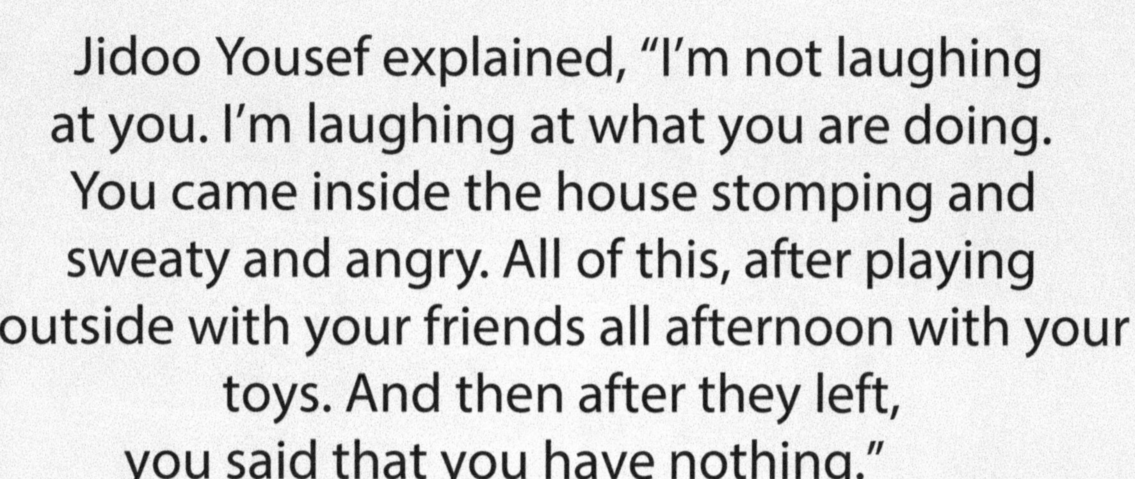

Jidoo Yousef explained, "I'm not laughing
at you. I'm laughing at what you are doing.
You came inside the house stomping and
sweaty and angry. All of this, after playing
outside with your friends all afternoon with your
toys. And then after they left,
you said that you have nothing."

"Yes, Jidoo, I have nothing. What do I have? And
you are sitting there laughing at me and playing
with those beads in your hands.
What are those?" asked Adam.

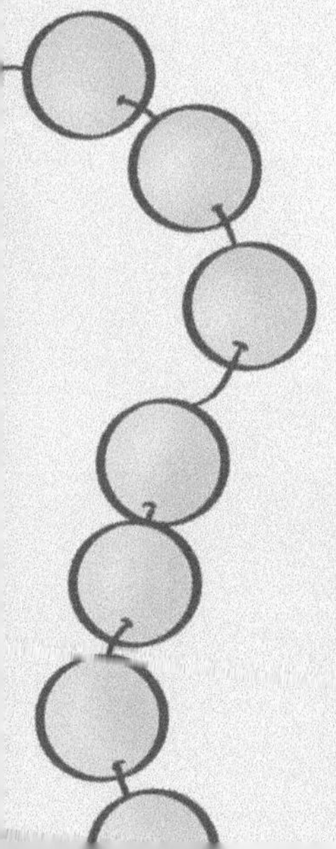

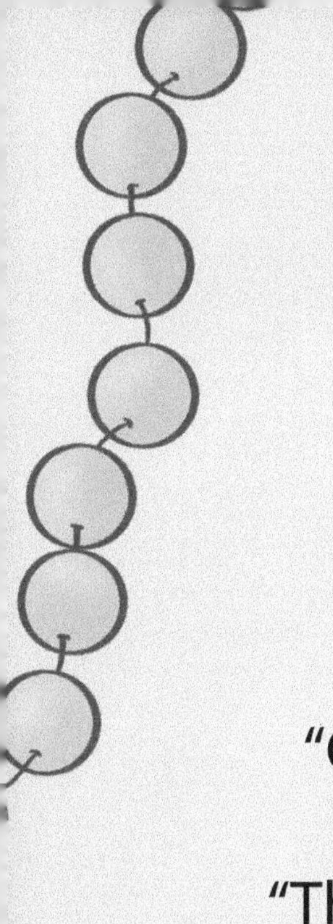
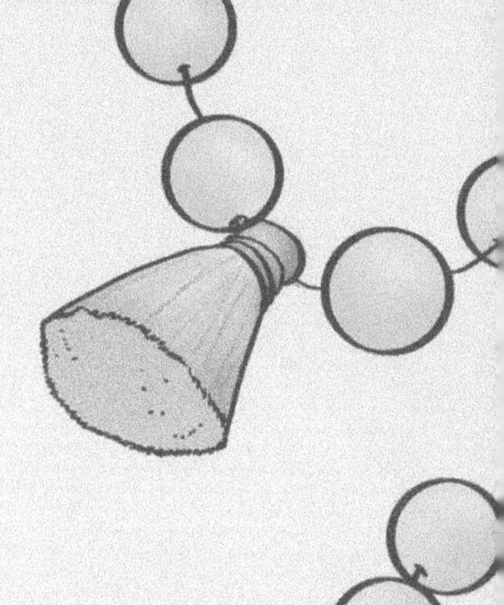

"Come Adam, I want to show you what these are." He held up the set of beads and said, "This is a masbaha. It has 33 beads. It is like the abacus you have in your room that you use to count things."

"Wow jidoo, it's smaller than my abacus and I can carry it around," said Adam.

"That's right Adam, it can be carried in a person's pocket. Some people use it to pray and give thanks to God, others use it to pass the time. Some people use it as a decoration in their home or car."

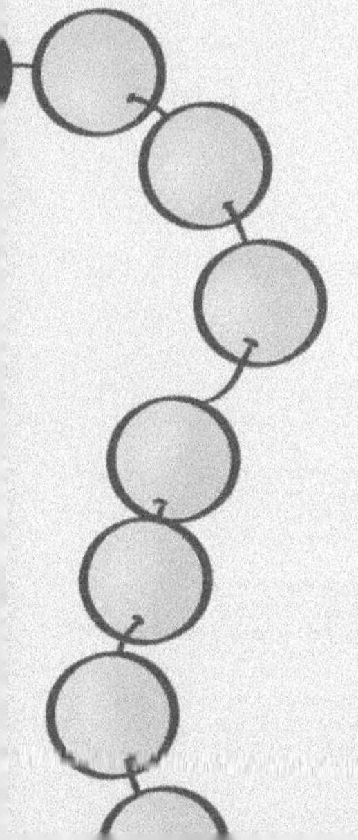
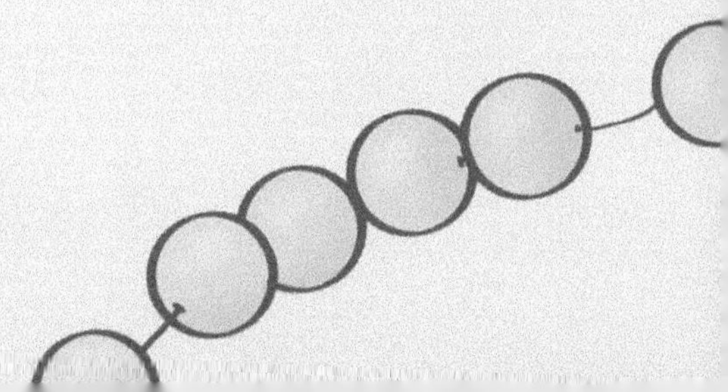

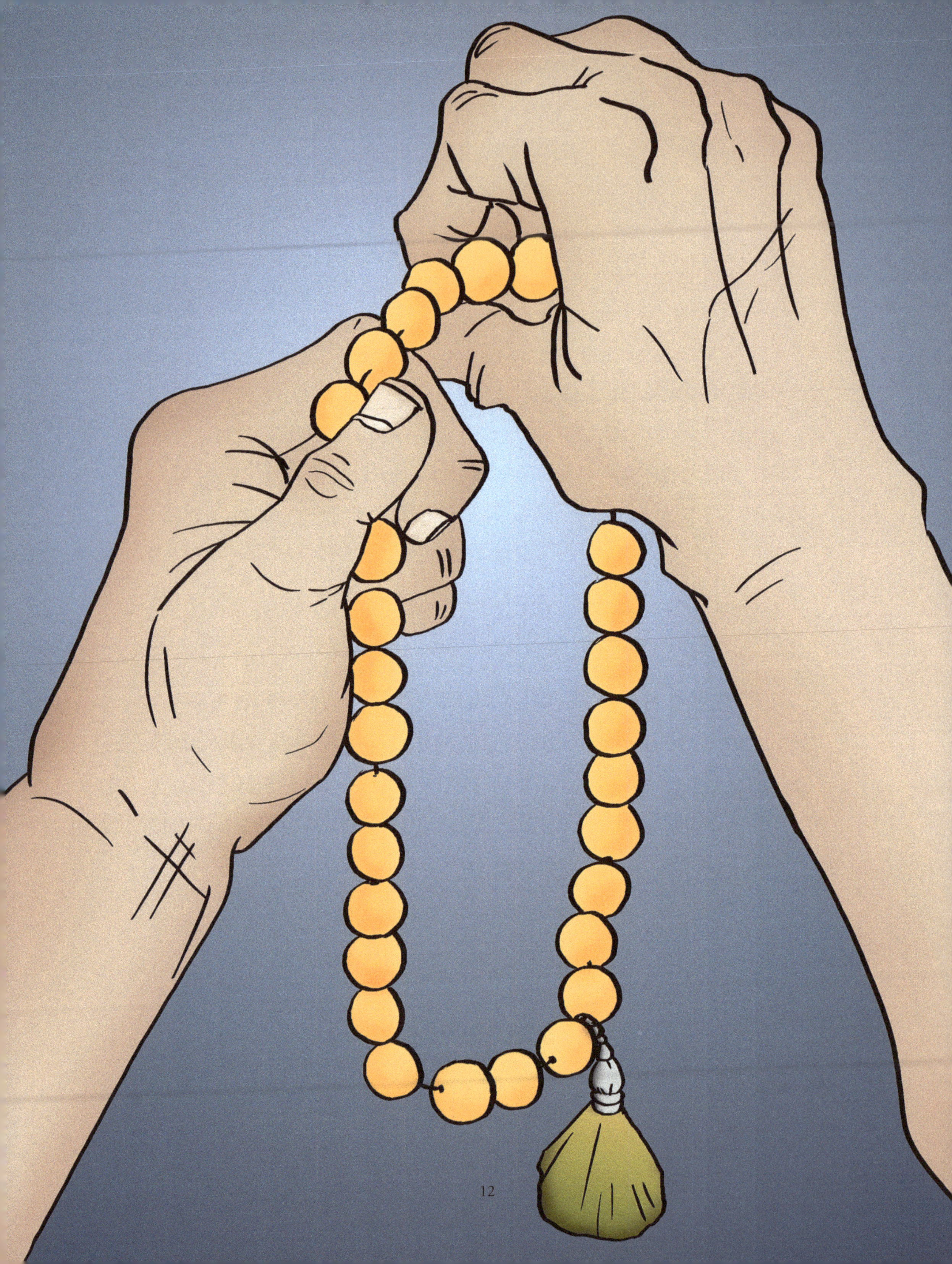

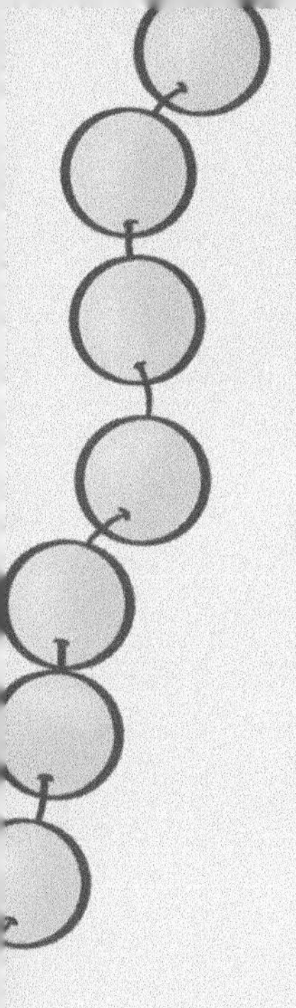
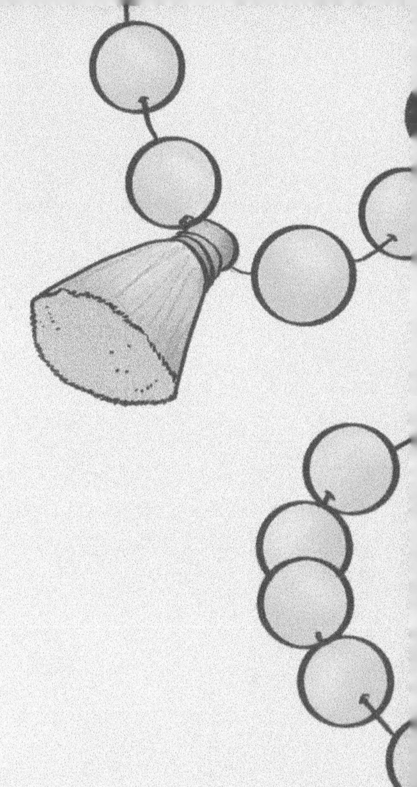

"How do you use the masbaha?" asked Adam.

Jidoo Yousef replied, "With each bead that I slide on this abacus, I thank God for a blessing that I have."

"What do you mean Jidoo," Adam asked?

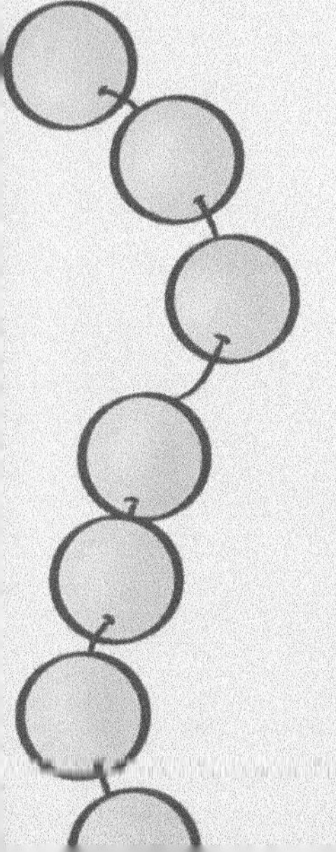
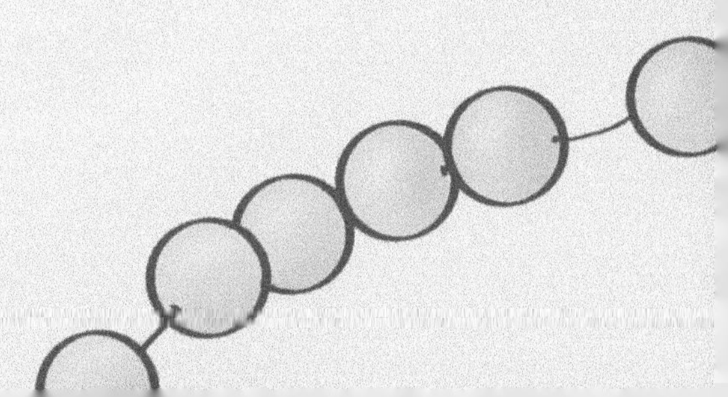

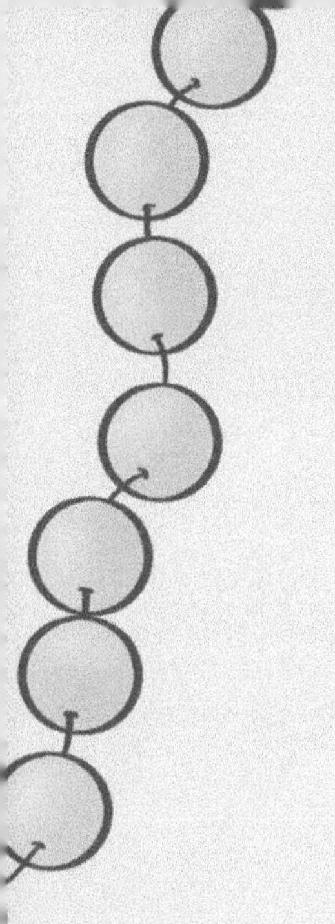
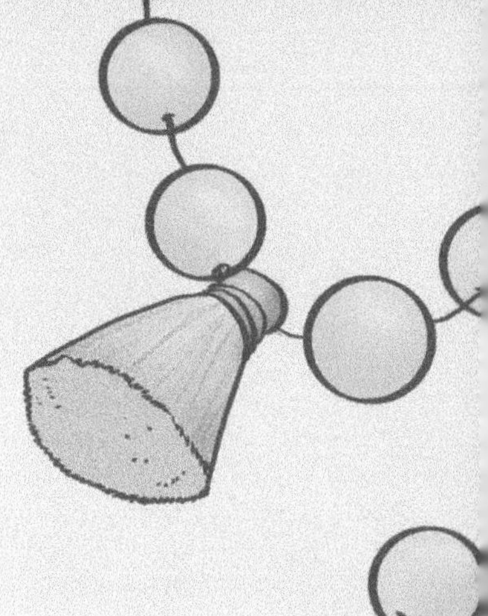

"Adam, you said that you don't have anything. Let's see if that's so." Jidoo Yousef took Adam to the front yard. Holding up the masbaha, he announced, "Let's count all the toys you have out here."

One by one they counted each toy until they reached the last one.

"Is that still nothing?" asked Jidoo.

"No! But," replied Adam.

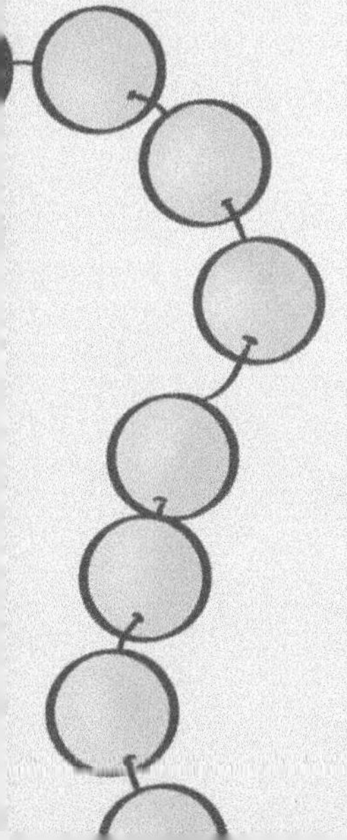
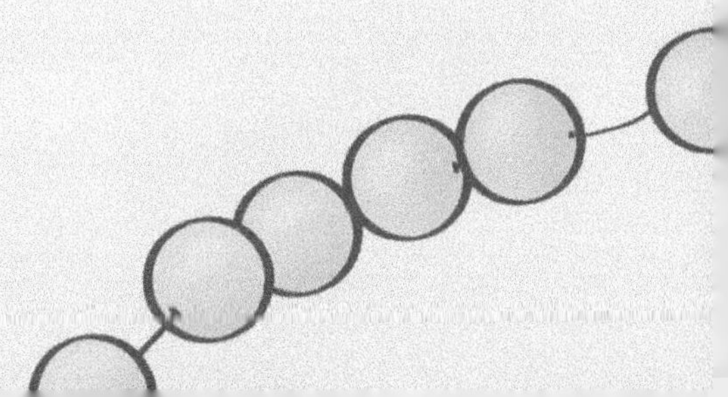

Then he took him out to the garden and began to count all the fruit and olive trees that Adam liked to pick from.

One by one they counted the fruit trees until they reached the last tree. Then one by one they counted the olives until they reached the last olive tree.

"Are those still nothing?"

"No! But", replied Adam

"Let's count the number of fruits on the trees."

"That's a lot!" exclaimed Adam.

"Yes, it is a lot!" agreed Jidoo.

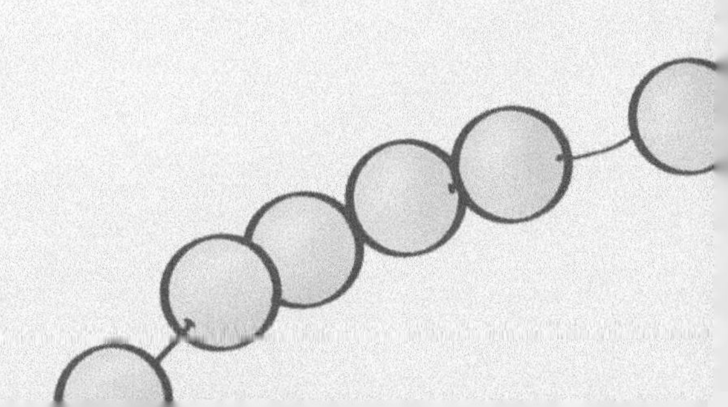

1
2
3
4
5
6

They moved on to count the number of houses in their neighborhood. One by one Adam counted all the houses around his grandparents' home.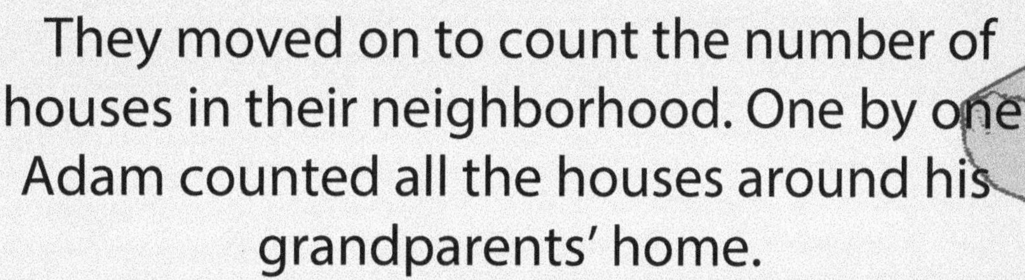

"Is that still nothing?" asked Jidoo.

"No! But," replied Adam

"Let's count how many friends you have there," said Jidoo.

One by one Adam counted how many friends he had in those homes.

"Is that still nothing?" asked Jidoo.

"No! But..," replied Adam.

"Let's count how many cousins and relatives you have," said Jidoo.

And one by one Adam counted his cousins and relatives. That was a lot.

"Is that still nothing?" asked Jidoo.

"No! I really do have a lot. I just never counted what I had!" proclaimed Adam.

"You are truly blessed Adam and I hope you will never forget that," added Jidoo.

Adam held up the bead on top of the masbaha
and exclaimed, "I have one more blessing to
count Jidoo -that's you!"

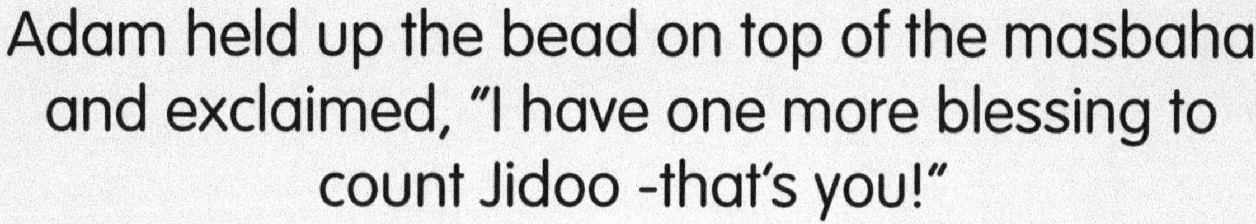

He threw himself into Jidoo's arms for a great
big, loving hug.

Adam and Jidoo smiled and hugged, knowing
that they were truly blessed because they had
each other.

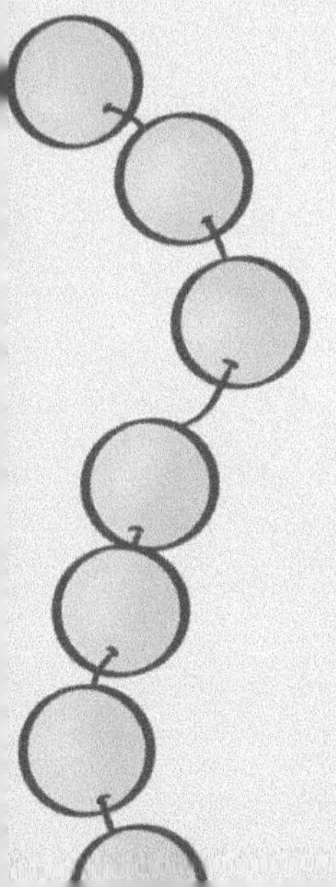

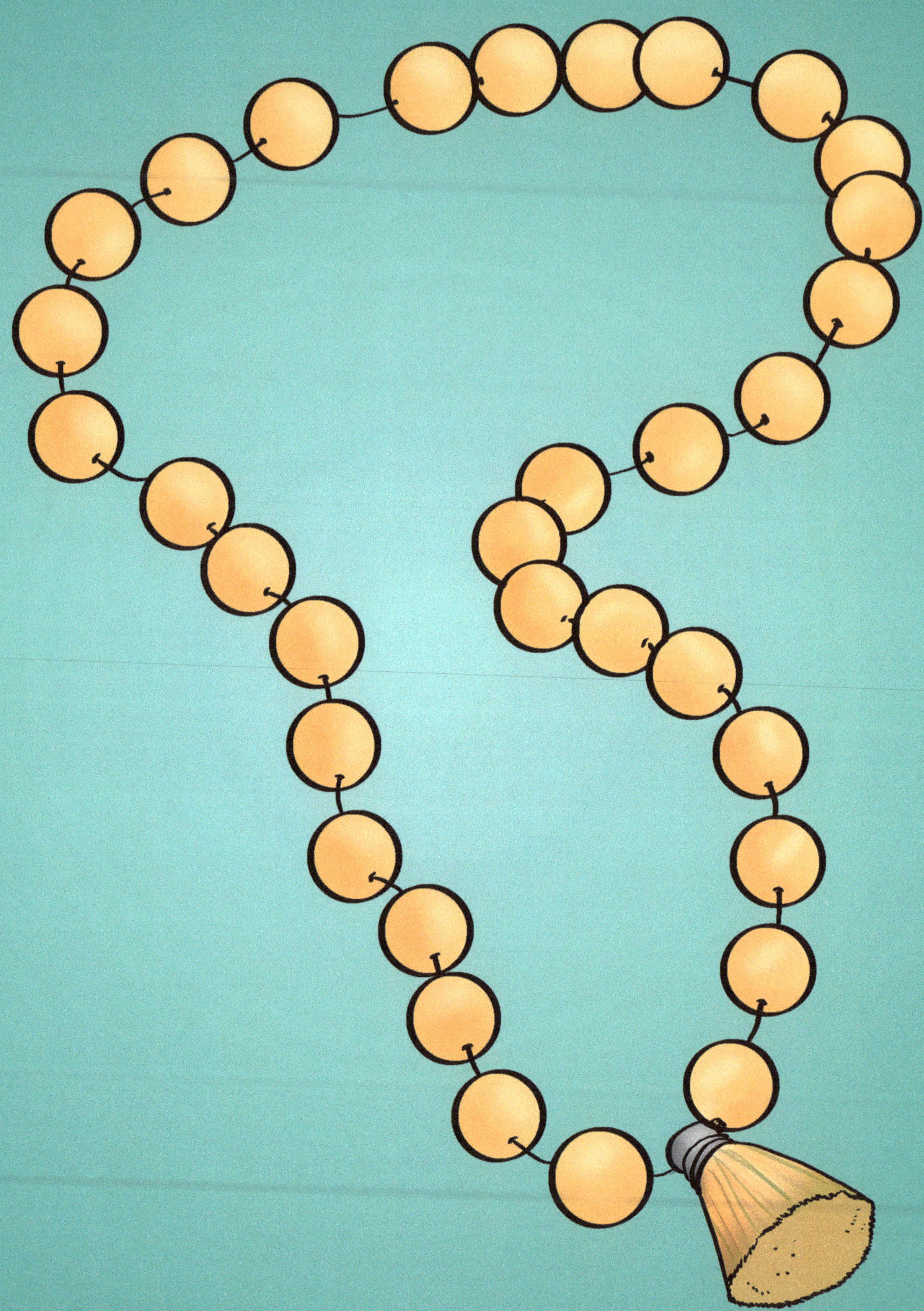

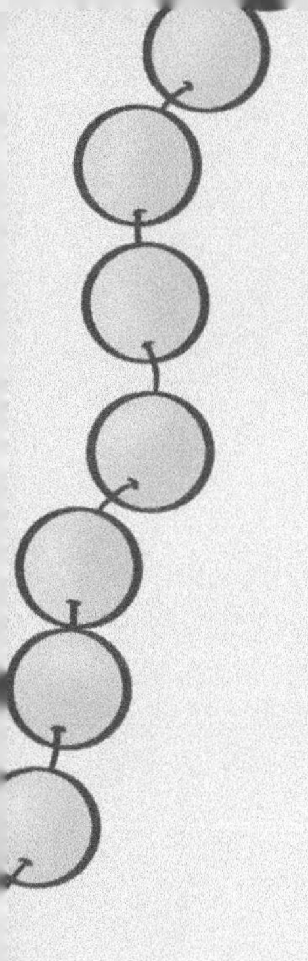
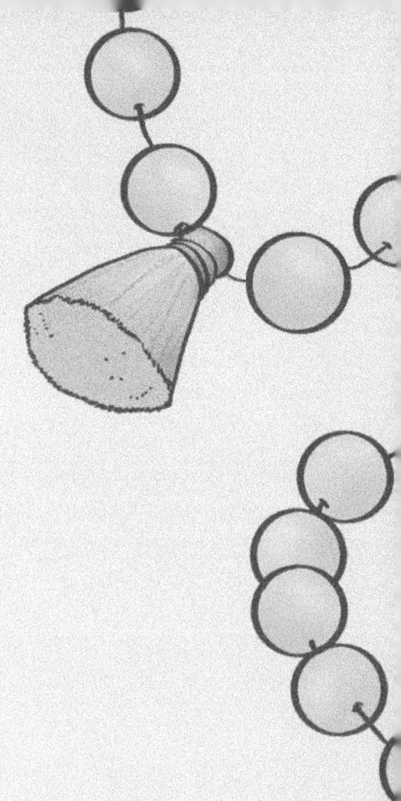

How many blessings will
you count using the masbaha?

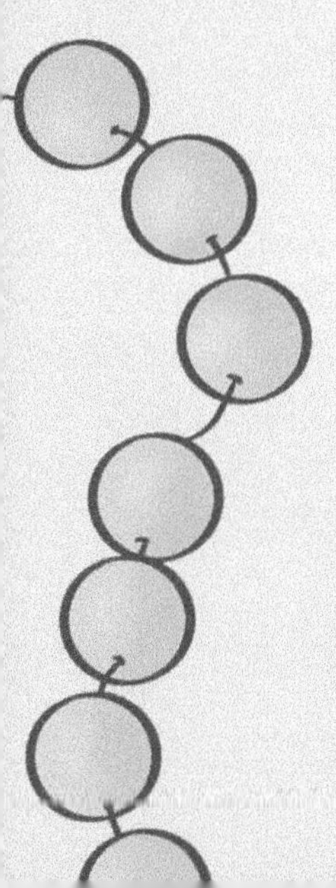
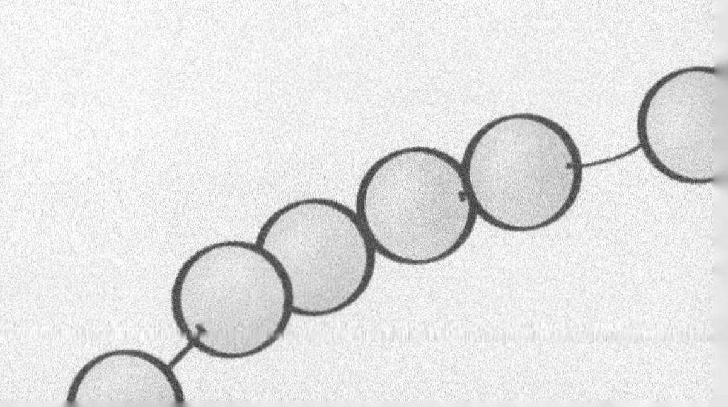